ABOUT THIS BOOK

MIGHTIEST OF MORTALS: HERACLES
Doris Gates

Heracles was the most famous hero in Greece. The son of
Zeus and the mortal Alcmene, he had unparalleled strength,
courage, and daring. Forced to perform twelve labors for
King Eurystheus, he battled terrifying monsters, captured
impossible prizes, and defied mortal tyrants. His adventures
took him all over the ancient world and finally earned him a
place among the gods on Mount Olympus.

Here also are the stories of:

Cerberus—the three-headed dog who guards the gates of Hell
The Hydra—a creature with a hundred flaming snakes' heads
Geryon—the cruel king with three bodies
The Nemean Lion—who had a hide no weapon could pierce
The Stymphalian Birds—with feathers sharp as arrows

MIGHTIEST OF MORTALS

Doris Gates

MIGHTIEST OF MORTALS: HERACLES

Illustrated by Richard Cuffari

Puffin Books

A Division of Penguin Books USA Inc., 375 Hudson Street, New York, New York, 10014
Penguin Books Ltd, Harmondsworth, Middlesex, England
Penguin Books, 40 West 23rd Street, New York, New York 10010, U.S.A.
Penguin Books Australia Ltd, Ringwood, Victoria, Australia
Penguin Books Canada Limited, 2801 John Street, Markham, Ontario, Canada L3R 1B4
Penguin Books (N.Z.) Ltd, 182-190 Wairau Road, Auckland 10, New Zealand

First published by The Viking Press 1975
Published in Puffin Books 1984
10 9 8 7 6
Copyright © 1975 by Doris Gates
All rights reserved

Library of Congress Cataloging in Publication Data
Gates, Doris, 1901–   Mightiest of mortals, Heracles.
"Puffin books."
Summary: Retells the exploits of the Greek demi-god
Heracles, including the tales of his twelve labors.
1. Heracles (Greek mythology)—Juvenile literature.
[1. Heracles (Greek mythology)   2. Mythology, Greek]
I. Cuffari, Richard, 1925–   ill.   II. Title.
BL820.H5G37   1984   292'.211   [398.2]   83-43166   ISBN 0 14 03.1531 4

Printed in the United States of America

*These stories are all dedicated
to the boys and girls
of Fresno County, California,
who heard them first*

CONTENTS

FIRST ADVENTURES

A Son of Zeus

It was night in a palace in Thebes, a city of ancient Greece. All within that palace were asleep and everything was still in the nursery where twin brothers lay slumbering in their single crib. The soft light of a small oil lamp hanging from a beam on slender chains revealed the faces of the sleeping babies and the figure of the slave girl lying motionless on a pallet not far from the crib. She was in a deep slumber or she might have caught the slight rasping on the stone floor as two large serpents came slithering through the doorway from the corridor outside. They lifted their heads, for a quick look around the chamber, their tongues darting in and out. They wriggled swiftly toward the crib. In a moment they were inside, and gliding atop the soft bedclothes, they stretched themselves toward the boys' necks.

Feeling the sudden tightening around his throat, one infant let out a lusty scream. But the other jerked himself up and, seizing the scaly coil wrapped around him, tore the snake loose and held it wriggling at arm's length. Then he reached toward his brother and grabbed the other serpent. Quickly the coils relaxed, and while the slave girl, wakened by that first scream, watched in helpless horror, the infant crushed each snake until its frantic squirmings ceased and it hung limp from his chubby hands, all life squeezed out of it.

Thus did Heracles declare his divine heritage, for he was a son of Zeus, who had loved his mother, Alcmene.

That one cry had brought Alcmene into the room. She gasped at the sight that met her eyes. The one boy, Iphicles, was still crying from shock and fear. But not Heracles. He smiled at his mother and flung the snakes away.

Another figure loomed in the doorway of the nursery, a tall figure, quiet and brooding. This was Amphitryon, husband of Alcmene and father of the twins. Or rather, father of Iphicles. A suspicion had come to Amphitryon on the eve of his return from war the previous year, a suspicion that Zeus had tricked his wife and him. As indeed he had. On the very evening that Amphitryon was riding toward Thebes, victorious after subduing his enemies, Zeus had appeared to Alcmene in the form of her beloved husband. Overjoyed at his safe return, she eagerly plied Zeus–Amphitryon with questions of the campaign. He answered her with kisses, which she gladly returned. When, later, the real Amphitryon arrived home, his wife was amazed to see him in full armor. He, in his turn, was surprised and hurt when she made no reference to his victory. When he tried to tell her of it, she replied that he had said all that before. So Amphitryon was puzzled until the twin sons were born. Was one a son of Zeus? Now as he beheld the snakes in the hands of Heracles, he had his answer. This was an undoubted son of the Hurler of Thunderbolts.

Early Training

Hera, wife of Zeus, had sent the snakes. She had known of her husband's infatuation with Alcmene and she knew when Heracles had been conceived. Her hatred of the child never abated. For the whole of his life that hatred was to pursue Heracles and bring him much torment and tragedy.

Yet Heracles was to become the most famous hero of Greece. In him could be found those virtues so valued by mankind, then and now: great courage coupled with physical strength, good nature, daring, loyalty, along with generosity. But as if to offset these fine qualities, the hero's nature also presented a formidable array of vices. He was lustful, quick to anger, gluttonous, and revengeful. (Still these are vices that mankind tends to forgive more easily than certain others, such as deceit, cowardice, and cruelty.) Since Heracles was free of these, his name rang throughout Greece as the embodiment of everything a hero should be. Many a boy took Heracles as his model.

Zeus knew this son of his was destined for greatness, and he planned that Heracles should have a kingdom suited to his prowess. Zeus knew when Alcmene's child was to be born, and he therefore decreed that the male child who was born within a certain time and of his blood should own the kingdoms of Tiryns and Mycenae. But Hera, hearing the announcement, found a way to trick him.

It so happened that the wife of Alcaeus, who was a son of Perseus, was expecting to give birth within a month or so. And since this would be a grandchild of Perseus, and Perseus was himself a son of Zeus, this infant would be as much "of Zeus's blood" as Heracles would be. All this Hera knew, and so she plotted accordingly. No sooner was the announcement made of the land gift than Hera sent her daughter, Eileithyia, a goddess of childbirth, to Thebes to prevent Alcmene's giving birth. At the same time she caused Alcaeus's son to be born immediately, thus robbing Alcmene's son of his inheritance.

For a whole week Eileithyia sat with her hands clasped on her knees. This was a magical stance, and while Eileithyia remained in Alcmene's vicinity holding this gesture, Alcmene could not bring her babies into the world. She might have died. But the mother of Heracles had a very clever maid-in-waiting. She had noted the goddess sitting within the courtyard of the palace, and it suddenly dawned on her what her attitude meant. Dashing from the palace on the eighth day, the maid-in-waiting cried to the goddess, "Rejoice with us. My mistress has been delivered of a son." This so astonished Eileithyia that for a moment she took her hands away, and at that instant the twin brothers entered the world. But Heracles, born a week too late, had lost the crowns of Tiryns and Mycenae.

Amphitryon, far from resenting Heracles, was a fond father to him. He knew this was no ordinary child and felt responsible for his upbringing. As soon as the boy was ready, he was given instruction in all the arts of warfare and hunting. He was instructed in music and boxing and wrestling. The best instructors in all Greece were obtained for him, and Amphitryon himself taught him how to drive a chariot.

The first sign of the quick temper that was to cause Heracles much grief came during one of his music lessons. Doubtless through the ages many students have longed to kill their music masters. Heracles actually did.

Linus was the name of the musician chosen to teach young Heracles how to play the lyre. Patiently at first, he showed the lad how to place his powerful fingers on the strings and how to pluck them. But Heracles was not the stuff of which musicians are made. He would rather be drawing a bow than plucking a lyre.

The day soon came when the teacher's patience

reached its end. It all began like any other music session. Heracles, clad in a white tunic, sat down sullenly on a low stool, his lyre balanced on his knee. Linus stood over him as if ready to pounce. "Begin," he ordered.

Heracles leaned the lyre toward him and promptly struck a loud discord. Linus grimaced like one in pain.

"No, no, you dimwit. Will you never learn to place your fingers?" he demanded in exasperation. "Here, let me show you."

He bent and none too gently placed the youth's fingers. "Now begin again."

Obediently Heracles struck the lyre, and another discord smote Linus's ears. Rage seized him.

"No one could be so stupid except on purpose!" he roared. "You are playing badly to humiliate me. I'll teach you to insult a son of Apollo!"

With that, Linus doubled up a fist and struck his pupil a hard blow on the jaw.

Not even wincing from that blow, Heracles sprang up with a snarl of rage and brought his lyre down on Linus's head. The music master fell to the stone floor, never to rise again.

This ended Heracles's music lessons. Amphitryon sent him away from the palace to herd cattle in the spreading pastures that lay some ten miles away from the city of Thebes. Here Heracles grew tall and strong. And it was here, when he had turned eighteen, that he met his first real test of strength and courage.

A Lion Hunt

Looming above the pastures where Heracles tended Amphitryon's cattle was Mount Cithaeron. It was densely wooded and was said to be sacred to Dionysus and the Muses. For some time Heracles had longed to explore its heights, but his herd-boy duties would not permit him to leave the pastures for so long.

One morning Heracles, while checking his herd, found the carcasses of two heifers that had been killed during the night, their bodies badly mauled. The meadow grass concealed whatever tracks there might have been. But Heracles, gazing up at the mountain, thought he knew who the killer was. He walked toward the slopes and came at last to where the pastures ended and the mountain wilderness began. Scanning the ground at the base of the slope, the youth found at last what he was looking for. In the damp earth bordering the little stream that flowed down from the mountain to the pastureland below was the clear print of a lion's paw. Plainly it was a big lion. It had come here to drink following its feast and was probably asleep now somewhere near the heights of Mount Cithaeron. Not hesitating for a moment, Heracles started to climb, his bow and quiver of arrows upon his back and a bronze dagger thrust into his belt.

The morning was fresh and fragrant. Birds darted among the trees and occasional birdsong broke the stillness as Heracles trudged upward. Every now and then he would stop and listen intently while his eyes tried to pierce the forest thickets. The sun rose; the trail, such as it was, grew steeper, and Heracles was glad when at length he came to a spring that gushed its pure waters out of a small grotto bordered with ferns. All about was shade and shade-loving flowers—violets and cyclamen. Heracles plunged his whole head into the cool fountain. He lifted it from the water and shook it vigorously as a dog shakes himself following a bath.

It was then he heard a faint cough. He froze, listening. It came again, clearer this time. Heracles sprang to his feet and swung the bow off his shoulder. He reached for an arrow, notched it, then drew the bow string taut while he circled slowly, trying to cover all sides of the glade.

Suddenly the quiet was rent by a fearful snarl. Heracles whirled in time to see a gigantic lion spring from a wall of green almost upon him. He loosed the arrow, but there had been no time to take aim, and it missed its mark. Heracles dropped the bow and braced himself to meet the lion's attack. The huge paws were reaching toward him, their claws extended. The gaping mouth was wide with roars, and the beast's fangs showed white against its curled tongue. Then the hero and the lion closed in a terrible embrace. Heracles locked his fists together upon the lion's shoulders and began to squeeze.

The lion's long tail thrashed the ground as the animal felt the awful pressure on his ribs. The roars ceased as he fought for breath. But Heracles showed no mercy. His arms kept tightening until there was the sickening sound of cracking bone and the beast went limp in the hero's arms. The fight was over.

Heracles, his chest heaving, looked long at the monster crumpled at his feet. Then he stooped, seized the tail, and began dragging his trophy down the mountain. He had proceeded perhaps half a mile from the grotto when he stumbled over a large fallen oak limb half buried in the side hill. He let out a curse, for he was wearing sandals and the sharp blow to his naked toes had hurt. He dropped the lion carcass, drew his dagger from his belt, and began digging out the limb. The wood was small-grained and hard. Heracles lifted the limb and swung it above his head. He grinned. Here was a weapon after his heart. He could stop any lion's rush with a swing of this stalk, he told himself. It would need to be fashioned into a club, of course, and for this an adz and an ax would be necessary, for no mere dagger could penetrate this wood. So, continuing down the mountain with the lion's tail in one hand and the oak limb in the other, Heracles at last reached the meadowlands.

Great was the consternation when it was learned that this youth had killed the lion no hunter had dared meet. And he had killed it with his bare hands! The herders were forced to believe the youth's story, for there was no wound in the lion's body and his ribs were certainly crushed. It was a feat for a god, they told one another, and they looked wonderingly upon this towering son of Amphitryon, a question in their hearts. But Amphitryon, when informed of the deed, smiled knowingly.

Skilled artisans went to work on the oak log, taking their directions from the hero who would wield it. When it was finally fashioned, it was an awesome weapon beyond the power of mortal warrior to lift and swing. But Heracles was half god, half mortal: a demigod. He swung the club easily above his head, roaring with delight at the sense of power he felt. Henceforth the club would be inseparable from him.

He carried it into battle when, some time later, the Minyans attacked Thebes. Single-handed, Heracles turned back the Minyan army. Creon, king of Thebes, was so grateful that he gave Heracles his beautiful daughter, Megara, in marriage. His younger daughter became the bride of Iphicles, the twin brother of Heracles. In time she bore a son to Iphicles who, when grown to manhood, would play an important part in one of the labors of Heracles.

The next several years sped by happily. Heracles and Megara were blessed with three sons. Then Hera struck again. It was too much for her jealous heart that this bastard of her husband's should have fame and fortune. She had tricked him out of his lands at his birth. Now she would succeed in taking from him something much dearer.

THE MADNESS

The Cruelty of Lycus

While Heracles was away on one of his long absences from home, a tyrant named Lycus murdered Creon and usurped the throne of Thebes. Megara, wife of Heracles, was Creon's daughter. Lycus knew full well that she, along with her sons when they were grown, would take revenge upon him for the death of their kinsman. Therefore, the tyrant planned to kill Megara, her children, and even the aged father of Heracles, Amphitryon, who lived in the same palace with them in Thebes.

The day of the killing was at hand, and the pitiful little family was gathered together on the terrace of their palace.

"Would that my son had never left this home to go to Argos and there try to win back my lands for me," said

Amphitryon. "When he departed he named me guardian of you and the children, Megara. I was to protect you from all harm. Yet here we sit awaiting death, and I am powerless to prevent it."

"You must not blame yourself," Megara comforted him. "There is no escape. The borders are watched. There is no one to defend us now that Creon, my father, is dead. Only Heracles could save us, and he is away without knowledge of recent events in Thebes."

One of the boys spoke. "Mother, why are you weeping and why does my grandfather look so sad?"

Megara put her arms around him. "The world is sad at times, and so I weep."

"Why are we gathered here?" asked another. "And what are we waiting for?"

"For your father's return," said Amphitryon.

"Is our father coming home?" asked a third son, his face suddenly alight with eagerness.

"We can only hope so," said Megara with a despairing sigh.

The sound of marching feet drew their attention to the courtyard in front of the palace which Lycus and a surrounding body of guardsmen were entering. The usurper's five victims drew closer together and watched his approach fearfully.

Lycus stopped and the guards dropped the butts of their spears with a clang upon the marble terrace. The tyrant looked over the little group with contempt.

"How can a heart so poisoned with cruelty continue to beat in your body, Lycus?" said Amphityron.

"I am not cruel, old man. I am merely taking precaution against the future," returned Lycus. "These boys will grow to manhood and seek to revenge me for the murder of Creon, their grandfather. And their mother, if allowed to live, in time perhaps could rally supporters around her and start an insurrection against me. And you might do the same, Amphitryon. I must protect my throne against my enemies. You are the first of my enemies, and so you must die."

"You could let us go across the border from Thebes and live as exiles in another land," argued Amphitryon.

Lycus smiled cruelly. "And you could slip back again across the border and cause trouble for me. No, you must die. Your deaths are the only guarantee of my throne's safety."

Megara had gathered her children close to her and now looked over their fair heads at their executioner. "And how will we die?" she demanded.

"By fire," said Lycus. "You shall be burned alive here at your own household altar."

He turned and faced the guards. "Go, men, and order oak logs hauled here at once." He turned back to his victims. "Your deaths must stand as an example to any others who may wish to rise against me," he explained, and entered the palace as if he owned it.

There was silence behind him for a few moments. The horror of his words had numbed even the children, who clung to their mother, white-faced and trembling.

"Now we can only pray," said Amphitryon. He raised his arms toward the sky. "Oh, Zeus, look down upon the

family of your son, Heracles. Attend their sufferings and save their innocent lives. Hear us, oh, Zeus, and succor us."

Hardly had the words left his lips when Megara cried out. Amphitryon turned to see what had caused her outcry. She was pointing, and laughing hysterically.

"Look!" she cried, her voice joyously excited. "It is he—it is Heracles!"

Amphitryon narrowed his eyes, the better to see where she pointed. "I can't believe it," he murmured. "It could be . . . I can't yet tell. Oh, Zeus, let it be true!"

And it was true. The boys broke from their mother and went rushing to meet the hero, who came striding toward them, his club on his shoulder, his bow in his hand.

He took all three boys in his great arms and hugged them. Then he looked toward the terrace, where stood his old father and his lovely wife. He saw the tears still wet on their faces, and the joy went out of his own.

"What's this?" he asked. "Why are you standing here outside my house, and why are your faces tear-stained?"

Megara threw herself upon him. "You have come in time to save us, my dearest! Now we will live."

Heracles held her away from him and searched her face. "Tell me quickly, Megara—who has threatened you?"

"Lycus," she said. "He has killed my father and taken the throne and has already planned our deaths."

"Dear wife, have courage. You need tremble no

longer. I am here to protect you against Lycus and the whole city if need be." With these words, Heracles released Megara. He went quickly across the terrace and entered his house.

They waited and soon sounds of struggle issued from within. Cries of rage and pain. Over it all came the sound of the tyrant's voice calling for help, help. Then Heracles appeared with the body of Lycus in his arms. With a mighty heave, he flung it off the terrace, and it thudded onto the pavement below.

"Now has cruelty been avenged," said Amphitryon. "We thank you, Zeus, for answering our prayer."

Hera's Dreadful Wrath

Hera was enraged by her husband's act of mercy. She determined that Heracles must be punished so terribly that never again would Zeus dare to help him. She had noted the hero's love for Megara and his sons. Very well, then by his own act he should lose them all. She would send a madness upon him that would drive him to destroy his own loved ones.

The body of Lycus had been unceremoniously hurled from the house in which he died; therefore the hearth must be purified. For this purpose, Megara and her sons had prepared the offerings when Heracles entered the room. It was at this moment that Hera sent madness upon him. As he watched his wife and sons going about their sacred duties, suddenly they appeared as enemy intruders to him. His face flushed, his eyes swelled in their sockets, and he let out a frightful roar.

"What are these enemies doing in my house, befouling my hearth?" he cried, grabbing the boy nearest him. The child, bewildered, looked up to see his father's awesome club descending upon him. In an instant the boy lay dead, his skull crushed. Megara cried out and tried to screen a second son with her body, but Heracles drew an arrow and shot it from his bow so straight and true that it killed them both at once.

The last son tried to conceal himself among some draperies, but Heracles's spear ended his innocent life. The madman next moved to slay Amphitryon, who had come into the room, summoned by the sounds of violence. But before Heracles could reach his old father, the goddess Athena hurled a rock which struck him on the chest with such force that he was thrown to the ground, stunned. While he was lying limp and helpless, Amphitryon bound him to a column until he should regain his senses.

For a while Heracles slept there, surrounded by the corpses of those he loved. Then he awakened, and Hera's terrible revenge was total.

He was first aware of the ropes that bound him. "What is this?" he demanded. "Who has dared to bind me in my own house? What weakness was upon me to allow it?"

"Ah, my son," said Amphitryon, kneeling beside him and untying the ropes. "How did you offend the gods that they should punish you so cruelly? Look about you and try to live with what you see."

Heracles looked about him. He saw the bodies of his sons and his wife. He saw the pools of blood upon the marble floor. He saw his arrow mingled with that blood, and slowly the truth was known to him.

The hero's grief and remorse at what he had done were beyond description. Like a wounded lion which crawls off into the brush, eyes glazed with suffering, there alone to endure his agony, Heracles stumbled from the hall to hide himself deep within the palace confines. There Amphitryon found him moaning helplessly like one in mortal pain.

"My son," he said, laying a comforting hand on the hero's massive shoulder, "hear me now and be comforted. A madness came upon you, sent by the gods and for what reason none can tell, least of all I, your father. What have you ever done to deserve such punishment?"

"I have killed before in a wrathful moment," returned Heracles.

"And suffered punishment for your quick temper. Besides, Lycus struck you first. You had provocation. For this deed today, there was no provocation. But you must not blame yourself. You loved your wife and sons —you would have given your life for them gladly. This I know."

"Yet I did kill them and I must atone for it," replied Heracles.

"What do you intend to do?" asked Amphitryon.

Heracles sat for a long time, head bowed, shoulders

sagging. Now and then a heavy sigh lifted his powerful chest. Amphitryon waited, his face full of pity for the suffering Heracles. At last the hero spoke.

"I will go into exile at once and thus avoid the curious and accusing stares of my fellow Thebans. But first I must be purified of my terrible deed."

"Wisely spoken," said Amphitryon. "And when you have done that, go to Delphi and consult the oracle in that place sacred to Apollo. The oracle will tell you what your atonement must be."

With sudden determination, Heracles rose and shook himself, as if throwing off the grief that was strangling his will to live. He adjusted the lion's skin around his shoulders and started from the room, Amphitryon in his wake. Straight to the bloodied hall Heracles led his father and there grimly took up his bow and quiver of arrows, fitting them to his back. Then he seized his club, and after an agonized look around at the bodies of his dear ones, he clasped Amphitryon about the shoulders in a powerful embrace.

"Old man, farewell," said Heracles. "You have served me well and given me good counsel. Now I must leave you, and who knows if we shall ever meet again? Pray to the gods that I may rid myself of the horror now upon me. Good-bye, my father."

Amphitryon, choked with grief, seized the towering figure of his son in his withered arms. For a moment the two stood clasped together. Then Heracles roughly freed himself and strode from the hall, for the last time.

THE LABORS

Sentence of Atonement

Traveling north and west, Heracles came at last to a
city named after its king, Thespius. King Thespius
greeted the hero warmly. He willingly performed upon
him the rite of purification which freed Heracles of the
awful blood sin weighing so heavily on him. He stayed a
night in the king's palace. But next day his conscience
still caused him great agony, and he decided to take
Amphitryon's advice and journey to Delphi to seek help
there. Delphi lay to the west of Thespius, about a day's
journey. It was the site of the most important shrine in
all Greece. Here stood the famous temple of Apollo and
within it the oracle through whom the god spoke. Here
Heracles hoped for a sentence of atonement. By fulfilling its requirements, he could balance his sins against
his sufferings. No amount of suffering would return

Megara and his sons to life again. But his conscience would be eased in the knowledge that gods and men would know the extent of his remorse.

The sun was low in the west when Heracles came within sight of the walls surrounding the temple. On his right loomed dark above him Mount Parnassus, its brooding mass mysterious in the fading light. To the west, an opposing range of mountains cast long shadows over a winding plain green with olive trees. Beyond lay the sea.

Instead of approaching directly the gateway to the temple, Heracles left the Sacred Way—the marble road to the temple—and struck out upon a path that led him to the very base of Mount Parnassus. In moments, he was at the Castalian Spring. This fine spring of purifying waters had been formed when the nymph Castalia, fleeing Apollo's amorous pursuit, was changed into a spring that would forever after bear her name. Heracles bent and scooped up a handful of the clear water and drank it. Again and again he dipped his hand in and drank. Then he turned away and retraced his steps to the temple.

He entered through the gateway and approached Apollo's shrine. It stood high above him, its columns faintly gleaming in the dying light. Resolutely Heracles climbed the long rise of marble steps to the porch. Passing between the columns, he entered the temple.

Its interior was softly lighted by a circle of bronze oil lamps resting deep in metal tripods that stood at regular intervals on the polished marble floor. In the exact center of the sanctuary stood a very large stone intricately carved. This was the *omphalos,* or navel stone, which marked the center of the earth. It had come to rest there many aeons ago when Zeus, curious as to where the earth's center was located, loosed his two eagles at the same moment, one in the east and one in the west. They flew toward one another at exactly the same speed, and where they met the *omphalos* was placed and the temple later built above it.

A priest of Apollo glided out of the shadows and approached Heracles.

"I have a question to place before the Pythia," the hero said, referring to the priestess who was the oracle. Her name, the Pythia, arose from the fact that earlier this shrine had belonged to another immortal who had kept within it a fearful dragon called Python. Apollo had subdued the reptile and taken over the shrine as his own. But ever since, his priestess had been called the Pythia, after the serpent.

The priest disappeared and shortly returned in the company of an old woman wearing the costume of a young girl. This was the Pythia, the priestess of the god.

Heracles told her briefly of his terrible crime.

"It lives with me day and night and I would rid myself of its torment. Either that or I must seek the deepest haunts of Hades where my soul in torment shall make amends for my sin."

The priestess gave him a long and searching look,

then descended by steep stone stairs into a vault beneath the temple floor where stood the tripod on which she sat while giving her oracles. The priest accompanied her. While Heracles waited, suddenly vapors began to rise from the narrow opening where the stairs went down. Higher and higher they rose until they touched the temple roof. Then a voice reached his ears. It was low at first, then rose to a nearly hysterical pitch of unintelligible babbling. Heracles listened carefully but could not interpret a single word. After a few moments the voice diminished to a mere murmur, then stopped. The vapors ceased to rise. The oracle had spoken.

After an interval the priest came slowly up the steep stairs and confronted Heracles, who stood tense now, his clenched hands holding his great club pressed hard into the floor in front of him.

The priest–interpreter spoke. "You can make atonement for the murder of your wife and sons by laboring for Eurystheus, king of Tiryns and Mycenae, for twelve years. If you perform successfully the labors he will lay upon you, you will obtain immortality and dwell forever among the gods."

It was a hard sentence, for Eurystheus was the man whose hastened birth had cheated Heracles out of his heritage. Now Heracles must become this king's bond servant or live in torment forever. For a silent moment Heracles stood stunned before the priest. Then, still silent, he went from the temple into the night.

The First Labor: The Nemean Lion

Though the distance in a direct line between Delphi and Tiryns was only some seventy miles, the waters of the Gulf of Corinth intervened between the two cities, so Heracles was forced to go double the distance across the Isthmus of Corinth and down into the Peloponnesus. He traveled night and day, halting only briefly for food and rest. It galled him to think of his meeting with Eurystheus, and he wanted to get it behind him as soon as possible. Moreover, twelve years of servitude was a long time. The sooner he could start it, the better.

After many days he came to the great fortress city of Mycenae. It stood on a rise that dominated all the plain, and his heart filled with bitterness at the sight of it. Eurystheus was king here, as he was at Tiryns, though he kept his court at the latter city. Trickery had got both kingdoms for Eurystheus, and now that injustice had been compounded by the sentence that made Hera's victim a bond servant of the unrightful king. As he thought of this, sudden rage seized Heracles, as it so often did. He cursed the city spreading above him, and he beat the dusty roadside with his club. But the huge granite blocks comprising the twenty-foot-thick wall surrounding the palace presented a stony indifference to the hero's bitterness. These walls, built by the Cyclops, could have withstood an army of giants. Their massive height seemed only a little less impressive than the range of mountains facing them to the north, from which summits, in centuries to come, watch fires would announce the fall of Troy.

His anger vented at last, Heracles continued along the road to Tiryns. Another eight miles brought him within sight of its walls.

Tiryns was a fortress city like Mycenae, only smaller. Cyclopean walls enclosed the base of a hill on which sat the palace of the king. Heracles strode up to the gateway, announced himself to the guards there, and was promptly conducted to the throne room.

Eurystheus greeted Heracles civilly. This was prudent of him, for the hero's sudden rages were famous and the king well knew this hero had a grudge against him. And even though armed men stood on each side of his throne, Eurystheus was certain that before they could subdue the giant standing sullenly before him, his own life would be forfeited.

When he had greeted him, Eurystheus asked what had brought Heracles to his kingdom and was told of the sentence of atonement.

"Something of this has reached my ears," replied the king, "and I have already decided on your first labor. You are to go to Nemea and there hunt and kill the lion which has been ravaging that countryside."

Heracles had not expected that any of his labors would be easy, but this command surpassed the bounds of all reason.

The Nemean lion, as he was known throughout Greece, was no ordinary beast of prey. He was the off-spring of two monsters: Orthrus, a two-headed dog, and Echidna, a repulsive thing, half nymph and half snake. A monster himself, the lion was indestructible. No weapons could pierce his hide; no club was stout enough to crush his skull. All of this flashed through the hero's mind as he listened to Eurystheus's command. For the first time in his life Heracles doubted his strength and ability; this task would most certainly be a test of both. But he revealed nothing of what he thought to the king. Never should this pawn of Hera's trickery suspect that any qualms had entered the breast of Heracles!

He shifted the lion's skin draped over one shoulder and belted about his waist, as if to say that he had hunted lions before. Then with a bow to the king that held more insolence than courtesy, Heracles turned on his heel and walked out of the throne room and out of the palace.

The labor that Eurystheus had laid upon Heracles had been well thought out, serving as it did two purposes. It removed him from the immediate vicinity of Tiryns—since Nemea was some distance to the north—and very probably it would remove forever this man who, Eurystheus knew, bore him no love. Such men were a threat to one's well-being as long as they were alive.

Now that he had entered upon his labors, Heracles took his time in going about the first one. Instead of marching directly to the plain of Nemea, which lay slightly north and west of Mycenae, he continued due north until he had reached the village of Cleonae. Here a shepherd named Molorchus joyfully welcomed Heracles into his modest dwelling. His own son had been killed by the Nemean lion, and now here was the mightiest of mortals come to destroy the dreadful beast. The shepherd never doubted that his son's death was about to be avenged.

The hero related to his host the story of Hera's hatred of him. He told of the madness she had sent upon him and of the oracle that had made him a bondsman of his enemy, Eurystheus.

When he had finished, Molorchus sprang to his feet, his patient eyes suddenly alight with enthusiasm.

"If Hera is so set against you, then we must propitiate her. This very moment I will seek out the finest ram in my flock and we will offer it to the wife of Zeus."

But Heracles dissuaded him. "Wait thirty days," he told the shepherd, "and if I return successfully from hunting the Nemean lion, we will sacrifice to Zeus. If I do not come back, then sacrifice to me in honor of what I attempted to do."

So Molorchus was persuaded and next day Heracles took his departure for Nemea.

He arrived at the Nemean plain around midday. A strange quietness pervaded the whole area. The sun stood directly overhead, poised before starting its descent into the west. No bird sang, no bee buzzed, no leaf stirred, and there was no sign of man or woman anywhere about.

"Are they all in their houses eating their midday meal," Heracles asked himself, "or has the lion destroyed every living thing around here?"

He considered approaching one of the peasant huts dotted about the plain. Its occupants might know of the lion's whereabouts. But he decided against it. The lion would have its lair where the hills started their gentle rise at the edge of the plain. Heracles started walking in that direction. He crossed a dry riverbed at the base of the rise and, forcing his way through the brittle brush along the riverbank, began to climb the easy slope under pines fragrant in the warm sunshine. He came at last to an outcropping of rock and paused for a careful look around. The rock proved to hold the entrance to a cave. Heracles inspected this opening. He saw darkness beyond the cave mouth. But farther back where no light should have been at all was a suggestion of light. Walking carefully, he circumvented the outcropping and discovered another opening at the back of the cave. He tore loose a large boulder and rolled it against this opening. If the lion should enter the cave, it would not be able to escape through its rear exit. Then, concealing himself in a clump of undergrowth, Heracles awaited the Nemean lion's return to its lair.

He waited several hours. The sun's chariot had journeyed well down the western sky, sending long shadows across the plain, when Heracles saw the huge lion approaching. It strode head down, its jaws bloody, its long tail stretching motionless behind the tawny body. It set its mighty pads deliberately, and its powerfully muscled shoulders moved smoothly with each cushioned step.

Cautiously Heracles rose to his feet. He notched an arrow to his bow, took careful aim, and let the arrow go. It struck the lion squarely and bounced off its impregnable hide. The beast stopped its slow stride to stare a moment at its assailant. Then with an angry roar that shook the ground, it charged.

Heracles met the charge with a blow from his club that should have crushed the monster's skull. The lion merely shook its head as if a bee had buzzed too close to its ear, and charged again. Again Heracles brought the club down, with no more effect than before. So when next the lion reared to seize him with the spread claws of its huge paws, Heracles moved inside its reach and seized it by the throat. The struggle that ensued tore up bushes and raised a cloud of dust that could be seen all across the plain. But when the dust had settled, the lion lay dead, strangled by the terrible power of Heracles' great fists.

Now the hero prepared to flay the monster. Its hide would be irrefutable evidence that he had performed this first labor. He drew his hunting knife and fell to work. But the knife could not penetrate the skin. Baffled by this fresh difficulty, Heracles sat back on his heels and considered what he should do next. An idea came to him at last, and, leaping up, he seized one of the beast's paws and cut it off. Using the claws of that paw, Heracles easily removed the lion's skin from the carcass.

When the job was finished, he flung the bloody trophy over his shoulder and set out for Tiryns and Eurystheus.

But first he must keep his promise to Molorchus. The good man was overjoyed to see Heracles and to know that now indeed his son had been avenged. He went at once to his flock and selected his best ram. Then he and the hero prepared the sacrifice to Zeus. When it had been accomplished, Heracles took leave of Molorchus and turned toward Tiryns.

Looking out from his palace, Eurystheus saw Heracles plodding determinedly toward the outer wall, the fearsome lion's skin across his shoulder. The sight so filled the king with terror that he jumped into a huge bronze jar to hide himself from the hero. He sent a messenger to meet Heracles and to warn him that from now on he was to report the result of his labors at the gateway to the palace and never to go beyond the walls.

In honor of his son's achievement, Zeus set the Nemean lion in the heavens as a constellation.

The Second Labor: The Hydra

This was the second impossible task. But Heracles was so encouraged by his victory over the Nemean lion that he felt less dismay as he heard the sentence.

The hydra was another monster born of Echidna but sired by Typhon, a creature with a hundred burning

snakes' heads. The hydra lived in a swamp at Lerna, a few miles west of Tiryns. It was a serpent with nine heads, one of which was immortal. The other eight possessed the ability to grow two back in place of each one cut off. As a companion, the hydra had a large crab which shared its swamp.

Heracles, too, had a companion for this labor. He drove to Lerna in a chariot, and his charioteer was his nephew, Iolaus, son of his twin brother, Iphicles.

They had hardly reached the borders of the swamp when the monstrous serpent came gliding up out of the marsh slime. Heracles sprang from the chariot and, drawing his sword, began striking at the many-headed snake. But as fast as one head was lopped off, two more grew in its place. Besides this advantage, the hydra coiled its lower body around the hero's legs, thus impeding his movements, and, to add to his difficulties, the crab crawled out of the marsh water and began nibbling his toes. Not even Heracles could cope with two such combatants.

"Iolaus!" he roared. "Come to me, come to me!"

In another moment he had stamped out the life of the crab.

Iolaus rushed to the hero's assistance. Immediately he saw the predicament that Heracles was in, and he dashed off and returned with a burning brand. Now, whenever Heracles struck off one of the hissing heads, Iolaus cauterized the stump so that no more heads could grow. One by one, Heracles struck them off until only the immortal head remained. This one, too, he finally managed to sever. He buried it deep beside the road, then dipped his arrows in the hydra's venomous blood.

The second labor had been accomplished.

Eurystheus, when he learned the hero was returning successful from his latest foray, popped back into his bronze jar, which he had lowered into the earth. From there he sent word that this labor would not count, since Heracles had had Iolaus to help him.

Not to be outdone by her husband, Hera, who had sent the crab, had it placed in the heavens as a constellation.

The Third Labor: The Cerynitian Hind

In the heart of the Peleponnesus, surrounded on all sides by high mountains, crisscrossed by numerous lesser ranges and watered by several fast-flowing rivers, lay the land of Arcadia. It was an enchanting region, the most beautiful section of mythical Greece, and a favorite haunt of Artemis, goddess of the hunt. Here she roamed the forest aisles, surrounded by her maidens, or bathed in the limpid pools laving the base of granite cliffs whose rugged sides in springtime were festooned with the bright blossoms of campanula and the green of fern. Here sunlight, slanting into groves of oak, turned the twisted gray trunks to silver, and here, lending her own beauty to the charm of bower and glade, lived the Cerynitian hind.

This most wondrous creature was sacred to Artemis. Unlike any other female deer, she had horns and they were of solid gold. Her hooves were silver. Since the hind was sacred to Artemis, it could not be killed, but it could be caught. For his third labor Heracles was commanded to bring Eurystheus this lovely hind.

It was not a dangerous mission, but it was an all but impossible one, for the hind, like all deer, was fleet of foot. For a whole year the hero sought her. Often he caught glimpses of her grazing daintily in an open glade or stepping delicately along a forest trail. He could easily have shot her with one of his poisoned arrows, but he must take her alive. He wandered futilely in search of her all over Arcadia, and some say he went as far as the region of the Hyperboreans, a people who lived in perpetual bliss in a land beyond the north wind.

The task seemed utterly hopeless, but, as sometimes happens in desperate undertakings, just when the hero was at the point of abandoning the search and surrendering to Eurystheus for whatever punishment he might bring upon him for his failure, Heracles came upon the hind asleep. She lay curled on the banks of the river Ladon on the western boundary of Arcadia.

For this hunt Heracles had provided himself with a stout net, the kind the peasants used for subduing wild bulls. Now he slipped it off his shoulder and, hardly daring to draw breath, approached the hind as she lay sleeping. With a practiced movement, he tossed the net, and it fell squarely over her. Jerking awake, she tried to get her forefeet under her, but Heracles was tightening the net against her struggles and she was forced to lie back, helpless. For a long moment the hero studied this quarry while the hind returned his gaze with fear-filled eyes. Then, gently for him, he lifted her off the grass and swung her across his shoulders. He was many miles from Tiryns, but with proper care he would get the hind there little the worse for her captivity.

Now it so happened that on this very day Artemis, accompanied by her twin brother, the god Apollo, was strolling along the banks of the Ladon. It was the hero's bad luck to come upon them, the sacred hind across his shoulders and its four feet held two in each of his great hands.

The goddess let out a cry. "How dare you take a creature sacred to me?" she demanded. "Release that hind at once or it will go hard with you."

Apollo sprang forward and would have seized the hind, but Heracles cleverly sidestepped him.

Artemis was reaching over her shoulder to draw an arrow from her quiver, her silver bow at the ready. "Drop it or I will send an arrow through your heart!" she cried.

Heracles carefully lowered the hind to the grass at his feet, but he tightly held the ropes of the net. "I intended no harm to the hind," he explained. "Great goddess, hear me now and have mercy on a most unhappy man."

The goddess's eyes flashed furiously and her mouth

was grim. "Mortal, speak quickly, for my patience is ebbing."

"It is Eurystheus, king of Tiryns and Mycenae, who desires this hind. It was a command he put upon me. I was to bring her to him alive, and for a year I have sought her."

Then while Artemis and Apollo listened grudgingly, Heracles began to tell of his madness, the curse that Hera had put upon him, of the death at his own hands of his loved ones. By the time he had finished, the eyes of Artemis were almost gentle, and a pitying look was on the god's face.

"Brave Heracles, promise only that no harm will come to the hind and you may take her to Eurystheus," said Artemis.

Heracles thanked the goddess. Apollo helped him place the hind again across his shoulders, and the hero continued on his way to Tiryns.

There Eurystheus, safe in his bronze hiding place, was informed of the success of Heracles's third mission. The Cerynitian hind had been brought alive to his palace.

In keeping with the promise made to Artemis, the hind was set free to find her way back to the safe confines of the forest of Arcadia.

The Fourth Labor: The Erymanthian Boar

The fourth labor assigned to Heracles took him straight back to Arcadia. It was not unlike the previous mission except that this was a highly dangerous one. Eurystheus ordered the hero to bring back to him alive a monstrous boar which had been ravaging that pleasant land, disrupting its harmony and endangering all who dwelt there.

The boar's lair was in the region of Psophis. On the way there, Heracles halted his journey to call upon a centaur named Pholus.

A centaur was a boisterous and unruly creature, with the body of a horse, except that where a horse's neck should be rose the torso of a powerful man with hands and shoulders. The centaurs had come to live in this region because they had been banished from their native haunts after entering into a drunken brawl at the wedding of a friend of Theseus, king of Athens.

Pholus was glad to see Heracles and welcomed him into his cave. Hastily he prepared meat and set it before him.

"Is there no wine?" asked Heracles.

A worried look settled on the centaur's brutish face. "The wine," he explained, glancing at a huge jar standing near the entrance of the cave, "belongs to all of us centaurs. We must use it in common."

"What nonsense is this?" demanded Heracles. "The wine is in your cave, isn't it? Open the wine jar, Pholus, and let us drink to companionship. Besides, what is meat without wine?"

Thus urged, Pholus lifted the lid from the jar and dipped up a cup of wine. But the scent of it was quickly caught by the other centaurs and they came surging into the cave, demanding their share.

A terrible fight followed during which Heracles killed several of the centaurs and drove the rest away. One, called Nessus, escaped to the river Evenus, where Heracles was to meet him again—to the centaur's sorrow.

Now, among these customarily brawling monsters was one good centaur. His name was Cheiron and he was a great teacher, famous for his knowledge of music and medicine. Many mythical heroes were educated by Cheiron, among them Jason and Achilles. Somehow Cheiron got involved in this brawl over a jar of wine, and an arrow meant for another centaur struck him.

Heracles felt awful grief at the accident and rushed to Cheiron's side and drew forth the arrow. But it had already been poisoned with the hydra's blood, and though Cheiron was immortal and could not die, the agony of his wound was more than he wanted to endure. He prayed to be allowed to die, and at last the Titan, Prometheus, bound to his rock in the Caucasus, agreed to assume the centaur's immortality and Cheiron was freed of his suffering.

With much mourning, Pholus and Heracles buried

the body of good Cheiron there near the cave in Arcadia, and Heracles continued his search for the Erymanthian boar.

He discovered the boar's lair on the high slopes of Mount Erymanthus. It was early in the year and snow lay deep upon the mountain. By dint of much shouting, he managed to drive the boar from his resting place and into the deep snow. Here the creature floundered helplessly and Heracles easily netted it.

As usual, when Eurystheus saw Heracles approaching Tiryns with the boar carried across his shoulders, the cowardly king took to his bronze jar and stayed in it until the hero had delivered his quarry and departed.

His next labor was delayed because of an expedition Heracles wanted to take part in. Word was brought to him that a hero named Jason was gathering a host to accompany him in a search for the Golden Fleece, a treasure held by King Aeëtes in faraway Colchis. This was adventure after Heracles's own heart and, taking a youth named Hylas with him, he departed for Iolcus where Jason's ship, the *Argo,* was being outfitted.

But during the voyage to Colchis, Hylas was lost on an island where the crew had stopped for the night. He had gone to find a spring of fresh water and, finding it, had been pulled down into the water by the nymph of the spring who had fallen in love with his beauty as Hylas bent to fill his water jar. Heracles, all but overcome with grief at the loss of the boy, left the expedition to go in search of him. When it became clear to the hero

that Hylas was, indeed, lost to him forever, Heracles
returned to Tiryns to take up again his labors for Eurystheus.

The Fifth Labor: The Augean Stables

Not unnaturally, Eurystheus was angry when Heracles took off for Iolcus without his knowledge or
consent. It was high-handed behavior in a bondsman,
and Eurystheus was determined that when next he had
an opportunity to name a labor for the hero, it would be
as humiliating a one as could be devised. The king had
by this time come to the conclusion that Zeus or another
powerful god was aiding Heracles and that no matter
how impossible or deadly the labor imposed upon him,
the hero would always succeed in executing it. So now
he was to be humiliated instead of jeopardized. For his
fifth labor, Heracles was ordered to clean the stables of
a certain king Augeas in a single day.

Eurystheus even chuckled as he gave the order. The
vision of the mighty Heracles carrying on his brave
shoulders baskets of stinking dung delighted the king.

With more patience than he was wont to show, Heracles accepted the task calmly and departed for Elis, the
country over which Augeas reigned. It lay some hundred miles west of Tiryns, and long before he got there,
Heracles could smell the stench of the Augean stables,

for they were filthy beyond imagining. King Augeas was rich in cattle and his cattle yards and stables had not been cleaned out in many years. So deep in filth were his pastures that they could no longer be plowed. And it was this mess that Heracles was to clean up in a single day.

The king was much impressed when Heracles was announced in his palace. He was even more surprised when he heard the hero's first words.

"Augeas, I have come to clean your stables which have long been a disgrace to this fair land," declared Heracles. "For one-tenth of your cattle in payment, I will clean them in a single day." He slyly withheld the fact that he was under orders to do so.

Augeas was amused at this preposterous boast and called in his son to witness Heracles's offer, easily agreeing to give Heracles one-tenth of all his cattle if he cleaned the stables in a single day. Then each swore a solemn oath to keep his side of the bargain. Heracles withdrew, smiling, from the royal presence. He already had a scheme in mind for fulfilling his side of the bargain.

Two fair-sized rivers flowed not far from the king's stronghold. One was the Alpheus, the other the Peneus. One coming down from the north, the other moving in from the west, their waters converged, flowing east just beyond the king's pastures.

The first thing Heracles did was to knock a large hole in the stone wall of the farthest cattle yard. Then he seized a shovel and began to dig at the nearest bank of the river. The sand and dirt and gravel that he heaved up with each heaped shovelful he threw into the center of the stream. And so furiously and powerfully did he work that before long, a dam began to form, forcing the water to the side of the riverbed and the breach in the bank. Suddenly there was a rush of water that tore a large gap in the bank, and the flood, moving swiftly on, gouged a new channel as it headed in the direction of the filth-filled pastures and the opened wall of the cattle yard. Mountains of dung choked the river at first, swelling its waters out across the pasturelands. But a great force was behind it, and always the water broke free to rush on across the pastures and cattle yards and stables of King Augeas.

By sundown all the filth had been washed away and only clean stones lay under the sparkling water. Then Heracles filled up the break in the riverbed by reshoveling the soil to where it had been in the beginning, and the waters of the Alpheus and Peneus swept along as they had before.

Once again Heracles stood before King Augeas, and this time there was no amusement on the king's face.

"Well, Augeas," Heracles began, "I have accomplished my side of our bargain. Your stables and cattle yards and pastures are clean. And the sun is not yet down. Therefore I claim my rights to one-tenth of all your cattle."

But the paltry king reneged on his bargain, even going so far as to insist that he never promised Heracles any such payment. This was more than his own son could endure.

"But, Father," protested the lad, "I heard you take a most solemn oath that you would pay Heracles one-tenth of all your herds if he cleaned your stables in a single day, and this he has done. Surely the gods will forsake you forever if you go back on your promised word."

This so filled the king with fury that he banished the boy from his kingdom on the spot. And he stubbornly refused to give Heracles so much as a single cow.

So Heracles left the country of Elis empty-handed and harboring a great hatred for the king. Years later he was to return with an army from Tiryns to sack the country of Elis and to kill Augeas. Thus was the king punished for going back on his word.

The crowning humiliation of this fifth labor awaited Heracles when he arrived back at Tiryns. Receiving the news from his herald that Heracles had succeeded in cleaning the Augean stables in a single day, King Eurystheus reported back that the labor would not count toward the hero's immortality because he had performed it for pay. History, even when mythical, is full of the duplicity of kings.

The Sixth Labor: The Stymphalian Birds

The sixth labor was the last to be performed in the Peloponnesus, and it sent Heracles back to Arcadia for the third time. He was to rid Lake Stymphalus of the hordes of terrible birds which had taken refuge there. The lake was surrounded by deep woods where wolves prowled, and it was to escape the constant threat of the wolves that the birds had flocked to the lake waters.

But these, of course, were no ordinary birds. Sacred to Ares, god of war, they were man-eating and bronze-footed and could shoot their feathers, sharp as arrows, into man and beast. They were a constant threat and nuisance, and now Heracles must get rid of them.

As he stood on the shores of the lake wondering how to overcome the monsters, suddenly Pallas Athena appeared beside him and put into his hands a bronze rattle which Hephaestus, god of the forge, had fashioned for her. Heracles took the rattle and the goddess vanished. He shook it vigorously, causing such a deafening clatter that the birds were filled with terror. They rose from the lake in throngs, crashing against each other in their haste to be gone. But before they could go far, Heracles seized his bow and sent arrow after arrow charging into them, killing hundreds and forcing the remainder to fly away. These landed finally on the island of Ares in the Black Sea, and there Jason and his Argonauts were to encounter them later on.

The Seventh Labor: The Cretan Bull

On ascending the throne of Crete, Minos had wanted to make a fitting sacrifice to Zeus in honor of the occasion. He appealed to Poseidon, god of the sea, to send him a sacrifice worthy of the Father of Gods. Answering his prayer, Poseidon sent a white bull out of the sea to Minos. But when the bull waded ashore and shook the sea foam from his white flanks, Minos decided he was too fine a creature to be killed. So he substituted his finest herd bull in place of the one sent by the sea god. Poseidon, furious at this betrayal, made the bull mad. Next, he caused it to sire a terrible monster called the Minotaur. For a long time now the white bull had been ravaging the island of Crete. For the seventh labor, Eurystheus commanded Heracles to bring the Cretan bull alive back to Tiryns.

Crete lay across the water a hundred miles south of Tiryns. When he arrived there, Heracles was greeted most kindly by Minos, who offered to help him catch the bull. But Heracles refused the offer.

"Help has already denied me one labor," he explained, referring to his struggle with the Hydra when

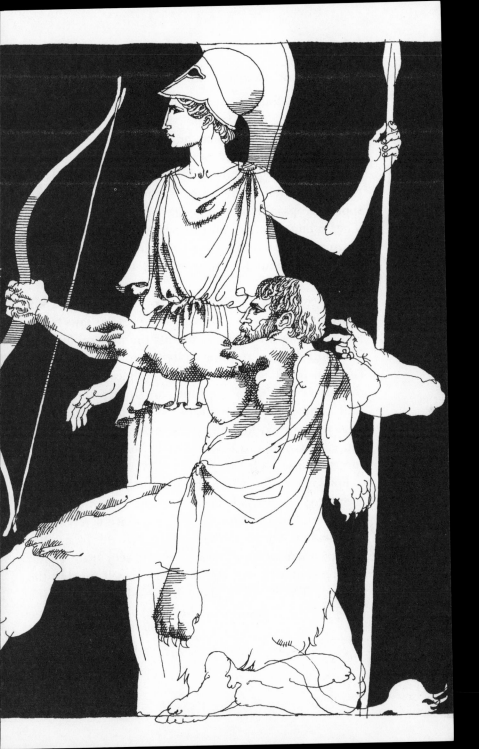

his nephew, Iolaus, assisted him. "If ever I am to win immortality, I must face my tasks alone."

So, shouldering his net, he started out in search of the Cretan bull. It did not take him long to find the creature. Every peasant and wanderer of the roadsides was eager to tell of the animal's whereabouts. And soon spoiled crops and torn hedges gave proof of his nearness. Then a huge cloud of dust thrown up by the mad bull's pawing told Heracles where his quarry awaited him. Heracles without hesitation started to where the dirt rose.

The contest was a short one. For an instant the bull faced his hunter with hate-reddened eyes, his jaws frothy and slavering. Heracles shook out the net and flung it. The bull charged, running straight into the net with terrific impact. The draw ropes were almost pulled from the hero's hands, but he hung on stoutly and let the bull rampage helplessly inside. When the monster had finally exhausted himself, Heracles dragged him to the shore, where he was loaded aboard the ship for the return to Tiryns.

For some reason which the ancients seem not to have accounted for, Eurystheus released the Cretan bull. The king would hardly have dared kill it since it was sacred to Poseidon. Nor would he have dared free it in another country than his own lest an army be sent against him. Whatever the reason, the bull was loosed outside the walls of Tiryns. From there he wandered out of the Peloponnesus, finally taking his stand at Marathon, near

Athens. Here it was that some time later the hero Theseus overpowered the bull and offered him as a sacrifice
to Apollo.

Thus ended the seventh labor of Heracles.

The Eighth Labor: The Mares of Diomedes

Diomedes was king of a barbarous country named
Thrace, far in the north of Greece. Though so far
removed from the haunts of more civilized men, Diomedes was famous as the owner of four man-eating
mares. Any stranger naïve enough to accept the hospital-
ity of this wicked king ended up tied hand and foot in
one of the bronze mangers of these terrible horses. Now
Eurystheus ordered Heracles for his eighth labor to cap-
ture these mares and return them to Tiryns.

Nothing daunted, Heracles set forth. Some say he
took a boatload of young adventurers with him. But
since the king had already penalized him for accepting
help, it is likely that the hero went alone.

Whichever version is correct, the results were the
same. Heracles killed Diomedes and fed his flesh to the
four mares. It had an astonishing result. No sooner had
they downed their master's flesh than they became en-
tirely docile. Though they had known neither bit nor
harness, they allowed themselves to be hitched to a
chariot and driven anywhere. Without difficulty Hera-

cles got them to Tiryns, where again Eurystheus turned
the quarry loose. Some say that descendants of these
mares survived up to the time of Alexander the Great.
Others affirm that the four wandered north on the trail
to home, as horses have a habit of doing, and ended up
on Mount Olympus, where they were destroyed by wild
animals. But Heracles had acquitted himself of his
eighth labor.

The Ninth Labor: Hippolyte's Girdle

Hippolyte was queen of the Amazons, a warlike tribe
of women dwelling at the mouth of the river Thermodon on the south shore of the Black Sea. She was
a daughter of Ares, god of war. No fiercer warriors than
the Amazons existed anywhere. They were the first
to use cavalry, and only Apollo could send an arrow
straighter than an Amazon.

Heracles was resting from his eighth labor when
Admete, the daughter of Eurystheus, requested an audi-
ence with her father. Since she was a favorite, it was
readily granted.

"Dear sire," she began, placing her hand in the one
Eurystheus extended toward her, "I have a favor to ask
of you."

The king smiled fondly. "I suspected as much."

"First I must know if you have yet assigned a new
labor to Heracles," she said, her eyes hopeful.

Eurystheus shook his head. "I have not yet decided what his next task will be. Why do you ask?"

"Because in that case, I have a task ready for him," declared the princess.

"Indeed?" The king looked amused.

"I wish him to procure the girdle of Hippolyte for me," said Admete.

Eurystheus appeared bemused at her words. His thoughts turned in upon themselves, and he did not reply to her at once. Admete waited, encouraged by his silence. The king was obviously considering her wish, possibly intrigued by it. Indeed, the idea which his daughter had implanted in his mind was not unwelcome to Eurystheus. This labor would be dangerous enough and profitable to his royal house if it succeeded. While, on the face of it, the recovery of a queen's bejeweled and golden belt might seem as humiliating a labor as the Augean stables to a hero of Heracles's stature, still the Amazons were a formidable host to go against. As a matter of fact, no sooner had he made up his mind to command this labor of the hero than Eurystheus determined to allow Heracles to take a complement of warriors with him. Since the girdle was known to hold special and highly desirable qualities for its possessor, the king wanted this labor to succeed.

Therefore, when Heracles departed from Tiryns, he sailed for the Black Sea in a ship containing some outstanding heroes of Greece. After several adventures along the way, they came at last to the city of the Amazons at the mouth of the Thermodon River.

To the surprise of the whole expedition, Hippolyte came aboard his ship and greeted Heracles most cordially. She had a respect for heroes, and the mighty strength and renown of the one who stood before her pleased the queen.

"What brings you to this kingdom, so far away from Tiryns?" she asked him.

Heracles looked most uncomfortable at her question. Diplomacy was not one of his strong points. His eyes fell to the golden girdle circling her slender waist. He longed to reach over and rip it off her. Yet in the face of her cordiality he hesitated to commit an act so crude. On the other hand, how did one phrase a request to a queen that she give up her girdle to a stranger? For what reason should she part with it? Heracles knew of none beyond Admete's vanity. He cleared his throat.

"Hippolyte, I have come here with my companions to ask a gift of you, but my rude tongue now fails me."

She smiled. "Know that I admire you, Heracles. Say what you will."

"It is this, then," declared Heracles. "I have come to take your girdle from you if you do not give it freely."

" 'Tis bluntly put," said Hippolyte, "and from anyone else, I would insist that you make good your threat. But you are a fighter, Heracles, a hero of great courage. Honeyed words are foreign to your lips. So I choose to overlook your blunt speech. I will bestow my girdle most gladly upon you as a reward for your immense heroism."

Heracles could scarcely believe his ears. This was

proving to be the easiest of all his labors thus far. Much too easy, decided Hera, who had overheard their conversation.

Disguising herself as an Amazon, the goddess went quickly throughout the city, proclaiming that Heracles and his comrades were planning to kidnap the queen. Her words had instant effect. The Amazons sprang to their weapons and rushed upon the ship. As they swarmed aboard, Heracles assumed at once that the queen had betrayed him, and he killed her on the spot. There she lay at his feet, her golden girdle sparkling and bright. But the hero had no time to snatch it then. The warlike women were all about the ship, fighting fiercely to avenge their queen. The Greeks were hard put to defend themselves at first. But at last the strength and valor of Heracles won the day. The last Amazon was hurled overboard and the ship slid out of the mouth of the river and into the Black Sea with Hippolyte's girdle safe aboard.

Before passing through the Hellespont, the victorious crew stopped at Troy, where Laomedon was king. He welcomed the Greeks as help sent from Heaven.

"A most terrible fate is upon me," he told them. "Because I refused to pay them for building the walls of this city, Apollo and Poseidon have sent a sea monster against me. It has been despoiling my lands. Now an oracle has told me that unless I sacrifice my daughter, Hesione, to this monster, they will send a plague upon my land, destroying all who live here."

Already the unfortunate Hesione had been chained

to a rock at the water's edge, awaiting the dread approach of the sea monster, even as Andromeda had awaited hers. And like Andromeda's rescuer, Perseus, Heracles was equal to this task. It was a terrible fight between the hero and the monster. At times Heracles had to leap upon the city's walls to escape the serpent's venom. Finally his spear went straight between the gaping jaws, penetrating to the monster's vitals, and the fight was over.

Now in exchange for his services, Heracles had received from Laomedon the promise of the gift of his mares. They were a handsome team which Zeus had presented him as compensation for his theft of the king's son, Ganymede. With the monster dead and Hesione safe, Heracles reminded Laomedon of his promise. But true to form, the wily king refused to make good his side of the bargain. His daughter was safe now! Just as he had cheated Apollo and Poseidon out of their wages, so now he cheated Heracles. The hero might have known that a king who would take advantage of the gods would hardly deal honestly with even the mightiest of mortals.

So now Heracles had no choice but to get aboard his ship and return to Tiryns with the girdle of Hippolyte. But he swore fearful vengeance on the tricky king and in later times made good all his threats.

The Tenth Labor: The Cattle of Geryon

His tenth labor took Heracles far afield, to the edge of the western world where Europe and Africa draw near to one another, nearly closing the western passage of the Mediterranean Sea. At this point, the hero set two immense columns, one on either shore. Throughout all antiquity and into modern times, the narrow entrance to the Mediterranean has been known as the Pillars of Heracles (or Hercules, as the Romans called him). Geographers know the passage as the strait of Gibraltar.

The purpose of his quest was to bring back to Tiryns the red cattle of Geryon, a monster who ruled over an island kingdom called Erytheia. Geryon had three bodies joined at the waist and thus possessed six hands and six feet as well as three heads. His cattle were famous for their great beauty and were much coveted. To protect them from thieves, Geryon had them guarded by a two-headed dog named Orthrus and a herdsman, Eurytion.

Heracles for some reason unknown to us took a roundabout way to the west, crossing the Libyan desert where the sun's fierce rays caused him to lose his temper.

"I'll fix you!" he shouted up to the sun god, Helios, at this time. "I'll show you what happens to anyone, god or man, who makes Heracles suffer!"

He jerked an arrow from his quiver, fitted it to his bow, and let it fly. Straight toward the speeding sun god's golden chariot it flew and would have struck Helios if he had not swerved the four fiery horses out of the way. The sun god was enraged at the hero's impudence.

"Let there be no more of that," he called down to the suddenly contrite hero. "I can wither you with one blast if I so desire."

Heracles realized that his quick temper had again almost been his undoing. He apologized most meekly to Helios, and to show his sincerity, he unstrung his bow.

The gesture pleased Helios. Besides, like all the gods, he knew that Hera was hounding the hero's life and making it a burden to him. The sun god's heart was moved to pity, and he offered Heracles his golden goblet to cross the water to the island of Erytheia where dwelt Geryon and his cattle. Heracles accepted the gift most thankfully.

Embarked in his golden goblet, he reached the island without further difficulty. There on a mountain slope he found the wonderful cattle and began herding them toward the seashore. When the dog Orthrus rushed upon him, Heracles quickly killed him with his club, and he dealt in the same way with the herdsman, Eurytion. He would have gained the shore and sailed away with the cattle without bothering the monster, Geryon, but another herdsman, guarding the cattle of Hades, ran to tell the king what was happening.

Immediately Geryon girded himself for battle. He

took up three spears and three shields and ran to head off Heracles. It was no true contest, for when the hero saw the monster charging down upon him, he sent an arrow straight through all three of his bodies. Then, loading the cattle aboard a ship, he set sail for Tartessus, where he returned the golden goblet to Helios and began the long journey home. Many adventures lay in wait for him, as people tried to steal the cattle from him.

One of these thieves was a three-headed fire-breathing giant named Cacus. Heracles had reached that place in Italy which later became the site of Rome. Night had fallen and he had halted for rest after watering the herd at a nearby stream. It was while the hero slept that the monster, already known and dreaded in the area for his thievery, seized two of the finest bulls in the herd and dragged them by their tails to his cave. Then he went back to the herd and stole four heifers. In the morning when he awoke, Heracles at once missed the six head of cattle. Like any herdsman, he assumed that they had strayed during the night, and he set about looking for them. He even crossed the stream to search for them, but they were nowhere around. Nor were there any hoofprints by which he could track them. At last, giving up in despair, he herded the cattle together and began driving them on along the way he had chosen as the route to Tiryns. By good fortune the way lay past the cave of Cacus. As Heracles approached with his herd, one of the stolen heifers started a gentle lowing. Heracles followed the sound and reached the cave, only to find an enormous stone blocking its entrance. It would have taken the strength of a dozen ordinary men to move it, but Heracles did not hesitate. He seized the stone and, strengthened by his own wrath, wrenched it away from the cave entrance. Deep within the cave's confines, Cacus sent streams of fire from his three mouths. Still Heracles rushed upon him and beat him to death with his club. Then he drove forth the two bulls and four heifers from the cave and continued on his journey.

Hera took a hand in the game by stampeding the cattle at once. Heracles had great difficulty in rounding them up again. When at last he did reach Tiryns and delivered the cattle to Eurystheus, it was something of an irony that the king sacrificed the whole herd to the goddess Hera. But Heracles had completed his tenth labor after eight years and one month of servitude to the king.

The Eleventh Labor:
The Apples of the Hesperides

The Hesperides were nymphs, daughters of Atlas. Their number is uncertain. Accounts vary, but there seem never to have been more than seven. The duty of these lovely maidens was to guard an apple tree that bore golden fruit. It grew in the garden of the Hes-

perides far on the edge of the western world where the
sun sent his last rays upon earth before plunging into the
western ocean. The famed tree had been the gift of Gaea,
mother earth, to Hera, when the latter was married to
Zeus.

All day long the nymphs danced singing around the
wonderful tree, aided in their watch by a fearful dragon
named Ladon.

For his eleventh labor Heracles was to bring to Eurystheus the apples of the Hesperides. It was an awesome
assignment for several reasons. To begin with, Heracles
had no idea where the garden was located or how to go
about finding it.

Wandering to no purpose, angry and frustrated, he
came at last to the river Eridanus. There some nymphs
informed him that the sea god, Nereus, could tell him
the way. They obligingly led Heracles to where they
knew old Nereus lay asleep and so could be easily seized.
It was necessary to lay hold of him because the old man
of the sea refused information unless forced to give it.
Moreover, he had the ability to change himself into anything he wanted—a lion, a snake, a bull, anything at all
that might frighten whoever had hold of him.

As Nereus felt Heracles's tight grasp upon him, he
awoke and struggled to be free.

"Tell me the way to the Hesperides," demanded the
hero.

But instead of answering, Nereus changed himself
into a huge serpent which wrapped itself around his

captor, writhing and hissing. Still Heracles held on. Next he had a bull by the horns which tried desperately to toss Heracles over his head, but the hero dug his heels into the ground and clung with both hands to the pawing brute. So it went until Nereus had exhausted all his roles and lay limp and helpless in his original form. Only then would he reveal to Heracles the way to the garden where grew the wondrous tree.

Thanking the nymphs and Nereus, Heracles started on his way, a journey along which adventures served as milestones. At one point when he had reached the Caucasus Mountains on his way back to the river Eridanus, a terrible sight confronted him. He beheld the Titan, Prometheus, chained to the mountain rock at the very moment when the eagle, which came each day to feed on the Titan's liver, was descending to his grisly feast. It had been foretold that one day Heracles would free Prometheus, who was being punished by Zeus for bringing fire to man, and now that prophecy was about to be fulfilled. Heracles notched an arrow to his bow and shot the eagle just as it settled on the shackled body. Then he struck away the chains and set Prometheus free. Grateful for his freedom, the Titan gave Heracles some advice as to how he could obtain the golden apples once he had found the garden of the Hesperides.

"Do not ask or attempt to gather the apples yourself," said Prometheus. "Rather ask Atlas to retrieve them for you. Atlas can approach the dragon with safety. What happens after he returns to you with the apples will depend on you," Prometheus ended mysteriously.

So Heracles continued west and came to the country of Libya ruled over by a king named Antaeus. This Antaeus was a famed wrestler and son of Gaea, mother earth. He took cruel delight in his prowess and decreed that any stranger entering his territory had to wrestle with him. And no man ever emerged from one of these contests alive.

Now it was Heracles's turn to wrestle with Antaeus. Sizing up the king opposing him, the hero had no qualms. The king was not overlarge, and however great his skill, it could hardly match the strength and skill of Heracles. But when the contest started and they gripped one another, Heracles discovered that he had underestimated his opponent. Now and then he managed to lift Antaeus off his feet, and whenever this happened, the king seemed to lose some of his power. But when Heracles flung him onto his back, he sprang from the ground stronger than ever.

At last it occurred to Heracles that of course the king drew strength from the earth. The earth was his mother! When next Heracles could get a good hold, he hoisted the king from the ground and held him there, slowly crushing the life out of him. Antaeus had wrestled for the last time.

On went Heracles ever westward to the coast of northern Africa, where the giant, Atlas, held the sky upon his shoulders. Here at last was the garden of the Hesperides.

Heracles flung his head far back to address the burdened giant towering over him.

"Greetings, Atlas. I am Heracles, come from King

Eurystheus in Tiryns, who desires your golden apples. I know the tree is guarded by a dragon who will not let me approach. But he will allow you to harvest all the apples you may desire. Will you get them for me?"

Now Atlas considered the golden apple tree his own. Didn't his own daughters guard it? An oracle had once told him that a son of Zeus would steal it from him, and now here was Heracles who might well be that very son of whom the oracle had spoken. Never would he have let Heracles enter the garden. But Heracles had asked him, Atlas, to get the apples for him. A wily look came into the giant's face.

"I can get the apples only if you will relieve me of my burden, Heracles," he said. "If you will take the sky upon your shoulders and hold it until my return, I will gather the apples for you."

Heracles considered. He did not want to assume the giant's burden. But Prometheus had told him to let Atlas get the apples, and he trusted the Titan's wisdom.

"Very well," said Heracles. "Place the sky upon my shoulders, but don't dawdle at your task. I am not as accustomed as you are to this load."

So the sky was shifted and Atlas, stretching mightily, went off to get the apples. After a while he emerged from the walled garden and approached the sweating Heracles, bowed under his unaccustomed load. The giant smiled down tauntingly at the hero's head.

"Make haste," said Heracles. "My legs are giving way under the weight of this sky."

Atlas laughed. "You will get used to it, as I did. For now that it is safe upon your shoulders, I have no intention of taking it back. But I will fulfill your labor, Heracles. I will myself take the apples to Eurystheus."

Heracles raged inwardly and cursed Prometheus. But then he put his wits to work. Perhaps this giant would prove to be as gullible as he himself had been.

"Wait, wait, Atlas," he called. "I came unprepared for such a labor as you have put upon me. Now take the sky back upon your shoulders until I have found a cushion to place on mine to ease the crushing weight."

Atlas returned to where Heracles stood and good-naturedly reached up and slid the sky back onto his own shoulders. "That lion's skin should do the trick," he said. "But make haste—I am eager for Tiryns and Eurystheus's palace."

Heracles scooped up the apples. "Farewell, Atlas. I will give Eurystheus your greetings." With these words, he turned his steps towards the east and in due time returned to Tiryns, his eleventh labor accomplished.

King Eurystheus decided not to keep the apples, however. He gave them to Heracles, who, in turn, presented them to Athena, who sent them back to the garden of the Hesperides.

The Twelfth Labor: Cerberus

His final labor was the most terrible of all. Eurystheus now demanded that Heracles descend into Hades and there seize Cerberus, the three-headed dog with serpent's tail who guarded the entrance to the realm of the dead, and carry him to Tiryns. Eleven dangerous labors had failed to dispatch Heracles. Here was one that would surely rid the world of him forever.

Mortal men had visited Hades before and returned to the land of the living. Most notable among these was the musician, Orpheus, who had gone to plead with Pluto, king of the Underworld, for the return of his bride, Eurydice. But no man went willingly into that dread realm peopled by the shades of the dead. And what man could hope to combat Cerberus and live?

In order to prepare himself for his visit to Hades, Heracles sought to propitiate the gods by being initiated into the Mysteries of Eleusis, sacred to Demeter. The high priest of the Mysteries, who had received his office from the goddess Demeter herself, initiated Heracles and purified him of all guilt in the killing of his enemies.

Following these ceremonies, Heracles journeyed to the southernmost tip of the Peloponnesus where the entrance to Hades was located.

The messenger of the gods, Hermes, was waiting to escort the hero into the Underworld. Wordlessly, the god led him to the back of a dark cavern shadowed from sunlight by overhanging cliffs. The god entered into the cavern's mouth, and drawing his sword from its sheath, Heracles plunged fearlessly after him. The shades fled in fright from the two, but one stood boldly up to Heracles. This was Meleager who, with Atalanta, had pursued the Calydonian boar. Heracles would have challenged Meleager, but Hermes drew him away.

"It is but a shade and harmless," he told the hero.

Next Medusa, the Gorgon, appeared before him, snakes writhing about her head. Again Heracles swung his sword, and again Hermes warned him that this, too, was only a phantom.

When they came near to the gates of Hades, they beheld two mortals seated as if frozen on huge stones. These were Theseus and his friend Pirithous. They were suffering eternal punishment for attempting to abduct Persephone, queen of the Underworld. As Heracles drew near them, they raised their arms most piteously to him, pleading to be set free. Not hesitating a moment, Heracles seized Theseus and wrenched him from his stone seat. But when he attempted to do the same for Pirithous, the earth shook so violently that the hero was afraid and released his hold.

So at last the hero came to the river Styx which dead souls had to cross in order to enter the kingdom of Hades. An old man named Charon ferried them over to where the dread dog, Cerberus, guarded the gateway. The frail boat almost sank when Heracles stepped aboard, so great was the hero's weight. He went past the chained Cerberus and into the throne room of

Pluto and his queen Persephone. They received the hero graciously.

"Why have you come here, Mortal?" demanded Pluto.

"To fulfill the twelfth labor that Eurystheus has put upon me, I must take to him the hound of hell, Cerberus. This I am determined to do even though I have to fight you for him."

"You are bold to think you can fight death and win," observed the king of the dead. "But a struggle between us will not be necessary at this time. You may take Cerberus to Eurystheus if you can subdue him without aid of weaponry."

Perhaps the initiation at Eleusis had not been in vain. It was not Pluto's habit to make concessions to visitors from the land of the living.

Heracles subdued the three-headed dog as he had conquered other monsters, simply by the power of his great arms. He crushed Cerberus in his mighty grip until the dog ceased to struggle and lay limp against him. Yet even then he tried to sting Heracles with his serpent's tail. The hero freed the dog's chain and led him out of Hades and straight to Tiryns. But when Eurystheus saw the two approaching, he hastened with all speed to his buried jar and leaped inside it.

"Take the hound back to Hades!" he cried. "I have seen enough of it."

So Heracles returned Cerberus to Hades and was free at last from his bondage to Eurystheus.

AFTER THE LABORS

The Glorious Victor

This was the title given Heracles after he captured and returned Cerberus to Hades. He had conquered death—the greatest victory of all. So great was thought to be the power of his name that superstitious folk put signs above their entrance doors warning all evil that Heracles was within the house. Since death was the greatest evil of all, it was hoped that Death would be stupid enough to believe the sign and pass on his way!

The hero was now free to settle old scores, and he lost no time in making good his threat to Augeas. This was the contemptible king who had gone back on his word and refused to pay Heracles his just reward for cleaning the filthy stables.

The campaign against Augeas was a hard one, for the king had two indomitable warriors on his side. These were the twin sons of Poseidon by Molione, who was the wife of the king's brother, Actor. They were inseparable in and out of battle. When they engaged in combat they both rode in the same chariot, one holding the reins and the other wielding the lash. They repulsed the first attacks of Heracles's army, and in one of them his brother, Iphicles, fell. Then Heracles was struck down by some dread disease, so that he could not lead his forces, and their morale suffered to the point that the campaign had to be abandoned. Besides, it was time for the Isthmian games when all combatants everywhere had to declare a truce.

When the twin sons of Molione started for the games, Heracles had them waylaid and killed. For this dreadful treachery he subsequently paid dearly. When next he assaulted Elis, the country of king Augeas, his forces were successful. The treacherous king was killed and Heracles placed Phyleus upon the throne. This was the son of Augeas who had remonstrated with his deceitful father when the king refused to give Heracles his pay.

The remaining order of events in the hero's life on earth is confused. But it is certain that he took part in the archery contest of Oechalia, and this led to other adventures.

The king of Oechalia let it be known that he would give his daughter, Iole, in marriage to the man who could outshoot him and his sons. This was just the sort of challenge Heracles would relish, and he lost no time in accepting the challenge of King Eurytus.

As might have been expected, Heracles easily surpassed all others in the archery contest. But when he
claimed his bride, King Eurytus refused him her hand.

"Heracles has won her according to your own terms,"
said his eldest son, Iphitus.

"That may all be," returned the king, "but I will not
bestow my daughter on a man who has already killed a
wife and sons."

This was a deadly insult, and Heracles raised his bow
against the king and his sons. He would have killed them
and Iole too if he had not been overpowered.

Again he was stricken with disease and journeyed to
Delphi, there to ask the oracle what he must do to be
cured. She refused to answer him, and this so enraged
Heracles that he seized the sacred tripod on which she
sat and started to make off with it. He would set up his
own oracle! But now the god Apollo, his oracle threatened, appeared suddenly and seized one leg of the tripod.
So they struggled, the god and the hero, neither giving
way, and neither able to overcome the other. At last Zeus
settled the argument between his two sons by sending a
thunderbolt which struck between them, forcing them
to drop the tripod. Only then did Heracles receive the
oracle he had come for. The priestess told him that in
order to be cured of his disease he must be sold into
slavery for a period of three years.

Now began for such a lusty hero as Heracles a humiliating chapter in his life. He was sold to Omphale, queen
of Lydia. She insisted that he don women's clothes and

learn all the domestic arts, while she arrayed herself in his lion's skin and even kept his club beside her. One can imagine the fury and frustration of the glorious victor as he went tranquilly about his spinning and weaving!

Free once more of his servitude, Heracles embarked upon many adventures. He even got together an expedition and sailed north to Troy to take revenge upon the king who had refused him the mares of Zeus as a reward for killing the sea monster. A noted warrior named Telemon accompanied Heracles on the voyage. And when the ships were anchored below the city, Heracles and Telemon breached the walls and entered it, Telemon in the lead. It so enraged Heracles that another man should be ahead of him that he raised his sword and rushed upon Telemon to kill him. Just in time, he saw Telemon drop to one knee and begin picking up stones.

The hero's curiosity was aroused and he lowered his sword. "What are you doing?" he demanded.

Telemon glanced up, a confident smile on his face.

"I am gathering stones to raise a monument to the glorious victor, Heracles."

Heracles, flattered and pleased, and accepting the tribute at its face value, allowed Telemon to live.

Together they conquered the city and killed King Laomedon and his sons, sparing only Podarces. Heracles gave Hesione to Telemon in marriage, allowing her to take whatever captive she chose with her. She chose her brother, Podarces.

"First he must be a slave," declared Heracles, "and then you must ransom him."

So when Podarces was being sold into slavery there before the ships, Hesione took the veil off her head and offered it as a ransom.

Thus Podarces remained in Troy and became its king. Later he would be known as Priam, father of Hector who would one day defend this same city against Achilles upon the plains of Troy.

Last Adventures

Another contest offered a wife to Heracles, and this time he was successful in carrying off his prize. He won the lovely Deianeira in a wrestling match with Achelous, a river god who wrestled in the shape of a bull. During the contest Heracles managed to tear off one of the bull's horns. Achelous recovered the horn by exchanging it for one of Amalthea's, the goat which nursed Zeus in his infancy. Amalthea's horn had the power of supplying food in abundance whenever needed. It was called the "horn of plenty."

The marriage had tragic consequences for Heracles. All unwittingly, Deianeira, in order to secure his love, caused his death.

One day when Heracles and Deianeira were traveling together through a lonely countryside, they came to the river Evenus. A centaur named Nessus had posted himself at the river's edge to act as a ferry to anyone wishing

to cross over. Heracles settled his bride on the centaur's broad back and himself plunged into the stream ahead of Nessus. All at once there was a piercing scream, and whirling around in the breast-high water, Heracles saw that Nessus was attempting to make violent love to Deianeira. He waited until the centaur had gained the farther bank, then notching an arrow to his bow, Heracles shot him through the heart. But as he lay dying, Nessus took fearful revenge on his slayer.

He called Deianeira to him and said, "You must take some of my blood and keep it by you for the day when your husband's love for you will be transferred to another. My blood will be a love potion which you have only to pour upon some part of his clothing and he will remain forever true to you."

With these words, Nessus died. Deianeira, following his advice, gathered the centaur's blood into a vial to keep for future use.

The time came when Heracles gathered an army and went to Oechalia to punish Eurytus for refusing him Iole. He killed the king and his sons and took Iole captive. Then he built an altar to Zeus to make sacrifice in gratitude for his victory. But first he needed clean garments, since a soldier's soiled raiment would be unsuitable for such a sacred occasion.

Now Deianeira had heard of the charms of Iole, and when the messenger arrived in Trachis requesting a fresh tunic for her husband, she suspected that he wished to make himself attractive in the eyes of his captive. The time had come to use the centaur's love potion. She took it out and plenteously sprinkled it over the clean tunic. While resting in the vial, the blood had become colorless and left no trace upon the garment. All unsuspecting, the messenger hastened away with it to Heracles's camp.

But when the hero put the tunic on, he felt a terrible burning all over his body. He wrenched the tunic off, and as he did so, large patches of his skin came with it. Nor did the burning cease. The pain was more than even Heracles could bear, and he begged to be put out of his agony.

In this terrible condition, he was taken by ship to Trachis, where Deianeira, on learning of what she had done, hung herself.

Heracles had himself carried to Oeta, a mountain near Trachis, and here he directed the building of his own funeral pyre. When all was ready, he climbed to the top of the pyre and laid himself down. He gave orders that it should be lighted, and a man, driving his goats past, kindled it. To him Heracles gave his bow.

When the flames had soared up and were about to consume the hero's body, a cloud appeared above him and Heracles ascended to high Olympus in the cloud.

Here he was received by Zeus, his father, and all the Immortals. Now he was a youth again and himself immortal. Zeus bestowed a bride upon him, the gentle Hebe, and Hera, her hatred of him at last satisfied, adopted him as her son.

And so the mightiest of mortals became one with the gods.

GLOSSARY

Achelous	ăk e lō′ us	Artemis	ar′ tĕ mĭs
Achilles	a kĭl′ ēz	Atalanta	ăt a lăn′ ta
Actor	ăk′ ter	Athens	ăth′ enz
Admete	ad mē′ tĕ	Atlas	ăt′ lăs
Aeetes	ē ē′ tēz	Augean	aw jē′ an
Alcaeus	al šē′ us	Augeas	aw′ jē as
Alcmene	ălk mē′ nē		
Alpheus	ăl fē′ us		
Amalthea	ăm al thē′ a	Cacus	kā′ kus
Amazons	ăm′ a zŏnz	Calydonian	kăl ĭ dō′ nĭ an
Amphitryon	ăm fĭt′ rĭ ŏn	Castalia	kas tā′ li a
Andromeda	ăn drŏm′ e da	Caucasus	caw′ ka sus
Antaeus	ăn tē′ us	Cerberus	ser′ ber us
Apollo	a pŏl′ ō	Cerynitian	sĕr′ ĭ nish′ i′ ăn
Arcadia	ar kā′ dĭ a	Charon	kā′ rŏn
Ares	ā′ rēs	Cheiron	kĭ′ ron
Argo	ar′gō	Cithaeron	sĭ thē′ ron
Argonauts	ar′ gō nawts	Colchis	kŏl′ kĭs

Corinth	kŏr′ ĭnth	Hellespont	hĕl′ ĕs pŏnt
Creon	krē′ ŏn	Hephaestus	hē fĕs′ tŭs
Cretan	krē′tăn	Hera	hē′ ra
Crete	krēt	Heracles	her′ a klēz
Cyclopean	sī klō pē′ ăn	Hercules	her′ ku lēz
Cyclops	sī′ klŏps	Hermes	hŭr′ mēz
		Hesione	hē sī′ o nē
Deianeira	dē′ ya nī′ ra	Hesperides	hĕs pĕr′ i dēz
Delphi	dĕl′ fī	Hippolyte	hĭ pŏl′ ĭ tē
Demeter	de mē′ ter	Hydra	hī′ dra
Diomedes	dī′ o mē′ dēz	Hylas	hī′ las
Dionysus	dī′ o nī′ sus	Hyperboreans	hī per bō′ rē anz
Echidna	e kĭd′ na	Iolaus	ī ō lā′ us
Eileithyia	ī lī thī′ ya	Iole	ī′ ō lē
Eleusis	ĕ lū′ sis	Iphicles	if′ i klēz
Elis	ē′ lis	Iphitus	if′ i tus
Eridanus	ē rĭd′ ă nus		
Erymanthus	ĕr ĭ măn′ thus	Jason	jā′ sŭn
Erymanthian	ĕr ĭ măn′ thĭ an		
Erytheia	ĕr ĭ thē′ ya	Ladon	lā′ dŏn
Eurydice	ū rĭd′ ĭ sē	Laomedon	lā ŏm′ e dŏn
Eurystheus	ū rĭs′ thē us	Lerna	lur′ na
Eurytion	ū rĭt′ i on	Libya	lĭb′ ĭ a
Eurytus	ū′ rĭ tus	Linus	lī′ nus
Evenus	ē vē′ nus	Lycus	lī′ kis
		Lydia	lĭd′ ĭ a
Gaea	jē′ a		
Ganymede	găn′ ĭ mēd	Marathon	măr′ a thŏn
Geryon	jē′ rĭ ŏn	Medusa	mē dū′ sa
		Megara	meg′ a ra
Hades	hā′ dēz	Meleager	mĕl′ e ā′ jer
Helios	hē′ lĭ us	Minos	mī′ nos

Minyans	mĭn' ĭ ans	Phyleus	fī' lē us
Molione	mo lī' o nē	Pirithous	pī rīth' ō us
Molorchus	mō lor' kus	Pluto	plōō' tō
Mycenae	mī sē' nē	Podarces	pō dar' sēz
		Poseidon	pō sī' don
Nemea	nē mē' a	Priam	prī' am
Nemean	nē mē' an	Prometheus	prō mē' thūs
Nereus	nē' rūs	Pythia	pĭth' ĭ a
Nessus	nĕs' us		
		Stymphalian	stĭm fā' lĭ an
Oechalia	ē kal' i a	Stymphalus	stĭm fā' lus
Oeta	ē' ta	Styx	stĭks
Olympus	ō lĭm' pŭs		
Omphale	ŏm' fa lē	Telemon	tel' a mon
Omphalos	ŏm' fa lus	Thebes	thēbz
Orpheus	or' fē ŭs	Thermodon	thur' mō don
Orthrus	orth' rus	Theseus	thē' sūs
		Thespius	thes' pi us
Pallas Athena	păl' as a thē' na	Tiryns	tī' rinz
Parnassus	par năs' ŭs	Titan	tī' tăn
Peloponnesus	pĕl' ō pō nē' sus	Trachis	trā' kis
Peneus	pē nē' us	Troy	troi
Persephone	per sĕf' ō nē	Typhon	tī' fōn
Perseus	pur' sūs		
Pholus	fō' lus	Zeus	zūs

ABOUT THE AUTHOR

DORIS GATES was born and grew up in California, not far from Carmel, where she now makes her home. She was for many years head of the Children's Department of the Fresno County Free Library in Fresno, California. Their new children's room, which was dedicated in 1969, is called the Doris Gates Room in her honor. It was at this library that she became well known as a storyteller, an activity she has continued through the years. The Greek myths— the fabulous tales of gods and heroes, of bravery and honor, of meanness and revenge—have always been among her favorite stories to tell.

After the publication of several of her books, Doris Gates gave up her library career to devote full time to writing books for children. Her many well-known books include *A Morgan for Melinda* and the Newbery Honor Book, *Blue Willow.*